Pat

Contents **Page**

written by Pam Holden

There are patterns in the sky.
The rainbow has a color pattern.
It is always the same shape.
What colors can you see?

There are patterns on the beach.
Shells have a shape pattern.
Some shells have a line pattern, too.
What shapes do you know?

There are patterns
on some animals.
Tigers have stripes
to hide in the trees.

Zebras have stripes to
help them hide in the grass.
What other animals
have patterns to hide?

There are patterns in the garden.
Flowers and leaves have patterns.
Spiders make webs in a pattern.
Insects have patterns on them, too.

There are patterns in numbers.
Look at a clock or a telephone.
Can you see a pattern in the numbers?
Do you know a counting pattern?
2 4 6 8 10 . . .

wall clock
this clock automatically adjusts for local daylight saving time
wall clock
STEWART everyday
ivy clock
wall clock
wall clock
wall clock
wall clock
wall clock

There are patterns in words.
Listen to a story or a poem.
Can you hear some words over and over
Can you hear a rhyming pattern?

There are patterns in sounds.
Listen to drums or a song.
Listen to animals calling.
Can you hear the same sounds over and over?

We all have a pattern of our own.
It is on our fingers — fingerprints!